Mr Wolf's week

Colin Hawkins

MAMMOTH

First published in Great Britain 1985 by William Heinemann Ltd. Published 1995 by Mammoth, an imprint of Reed Books Ltd, Michelin House, 81 Fulham Road, London SW3 6RB and Auckland, Melbourne, Singapore and Toronto. Copyright © Colin Hawkins 1985. ISBN 0 7497 2511 7. A CIP catalogue record for this title is available from the British Library. Produced by Mandarin Offset Ltd. Printed and bound in Hong Kong.

Monday is wet.
Mr Wolf puts
on his raincoat
and rubber
boots, takes
his umbrella . . .

. . . and strides out in the rain.

Tuesday is foggy.
Mr Wolf puts on
his checked coat,
yellow scarf and
red cap . . .

. . . and gets lost.

Wednesday is cold. Mr Wolf puts on a warm sweater, a scarf, mittens and two pairs of socks . . .

. . . and goes ice skating.

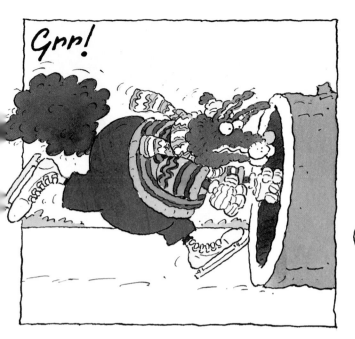

Grr!

Grr!

Grr

Thursday is snowy.
Mr Wolf puts on his
overcoat, gloves,
a woollen hat and
boots . . .

. . . and stomps out in the snow.

Friday is windy.
Mr Wolf puts on
his red jacket and
yellow trousers . . .

. . . and flies his kite.

Saturday is sunny.
Mr Wolf puts on
his jogging suit . . .

. . . and goes for a run.

CRASH!!

Sunday is very,
very hot.
Mr Wolf puts
on his shorts
and sunglasses . . .

. . . and heads for the beach.

AND THEN . . .

... it's Monday again!

Then Tuesday ...

then Wednesday ...

then Thursday

then Friday ...

then Saturday ...

then Sunday.

.. Another week is over ...

...and then it's Monday again!